rewind

Mark DOWLING

Copyright © [2025] Mark Dowling
All rights reserved.

No part of this publication may be reproduced, stored in a retrieval system, or transmitted in any form or by any means , electronic, mechanical, photocopying, recording, or otherwise , without the prior written permission of the author, except in the case of brief quotations used in critical articles or reviews.

This is a work of fiction. Any resemblance to actual persons, living or dead, or actual events is purely coincidental.

Contents

Chapter 1 : Careless Whisper 1

Chapter 2 : The Only Way Is Up 9

Chapter 3: Two Tribes 17

Chapter 4 : Too Shy 25

Chapter 5 : DeDoDoDo DeDaDaDa 31

Chapter 6 : Bohemian Rhapsody 37

Chapter 7 : Pretty in Pink 43

Chapter 8 : Last Christmas 49

Chapter 9 : Alive and Kicking 53

Chapter 10 : Lady in Red 57

Chapter 11 : Put 'em Under Pressure 63

Chapter 12 : Je T'aime 67

Chapter 13 : Saturday Night 73

Chapter 14 : Our House 79

Chapter 15 : Take My Breath Away 85

Chapter 16 : Eye Of The Tiger 89

Chapter 17 West End Girls 93

Chapter 18 : Walking In My Shoes 97

Chapter 19 : Heroes 101

Chapter 20 : Being Boring 105

Author's Note

Rewind is a work of fiction , though at times, it may feel like memoir, especially to anyone whose youth was lived in the '80s or '90s.

It's told in the voice of a man reflecting on the nights out, songs, friendships, and near, misses that shaped his life. But as the story unfolds, you may notice something else happening: his memories begin to blur, repeat, and shift. Time folds in on itself. The past starts to feel more present than the present.

He doesn't fully realise it , but perhaps you, the reader, will.

This isn't a clinical story about Alzheimer's or dementia. It's a personal, emotional one , about how memory works, how it fails us, and how sometimes the smallest moments leave the biggest marks.

As you read, I invite you to pay attention to the cracks between the stories , the silences, the loops, the things that seem almost *too* familiar. They matter.

Rewind is about what it means to remember , and maybe, what it means when we begin to forget.

Thank you for reading,
Mark

Chapter 1 : Careless Whisper

It's a funny thing, isn't it? You spend your whole life plodding along, head down, making the best of whatever falls your way. The job you landed into because it was there. The nights out where you laughed yourself sick and thought it'd never end. The weekends that blurred together in a mess of pints and plans and dreaming about winning the lotto. (Still waiting on that, by the way.)

And yet, now after everything , the only thing you really want isn't money, or a big house, or some fancy car. It's time. Just a little bit of time. A few stolen hours to go back and relive the bits you didn't even know were precious at the time. Not the big stuff. Not the life changing moments. Just the little ones. The ones that , looking back , were everything.

I was thinking all that and more sitting in the kitchen one Tuesday night. One of those never ending ones, rain lashing the windows, wind, you know, blowing litter all around. The telly was off. Lights low. Just the hum of the fridge and the tick, tick of the old clock on the wall telling me to go to bed.

Wasn't even properly tired , just that kind of worn, out only a fella gets from a lifetime of working, hoping, and waiting. I took a sip of tea. Cold for probably half an hour, but I drank it anyway.

And I thought about her.

Not the woman I'd married , God love her, she's got her own part in my story, but that's not tonight's memory. Not my mother, though she'd raised me with more heart than cash, and not the lads I'd grown up with either.

No, tonight my mind wandered back uninvited to her. The girl. The one who had once, briefly, looked at me like I was something special.

The Galaxy Club had been our stomping ground back then. A half step up from a cattle mart and only half as clean, but it was ours. Cheap beer. Smoky air. Shiny shirts and the smell of chipper vans wafting through the fire doors. God, we thought we were gods in there. A bunch of daft, broke lads, throwing shapes on the sticky dancefloor and hoping praying that we'd somehow catch the eye of someone far too good for us.

And that night ,that night , I had caught her eye. Only thing was, I'd bottled it. Stood there like a right eejit all night, nursing warm drinks and working up the nerve to ask her to dance. Waited until the very last slow set, the very last song, to make my move.

"Careless Whisper" was already halfway through before I finally got up the courage. . By the time I leaned in, heart hammering so loud I couldn't hear the music, she was already moving towards the exit with her mates. I caught her hand , barely , and asked, stuttering, if she wanted to dance. She smiled, that sweet, pitying smile beautiful women keep for hopeful lads, and said, "Another time, maybe." I nodded. Watched her disappear into the downtown lights .

Later, one of her friends , half drunk and chatty , told me the truth: "She would've said yes at the very first song if you'd asked. She was waiting for you, you know."

That stuck with me. Still does, some nights. And tonight, in the small hours, it dug its teeth into me harder than ever. Funny the things you remember. Half the time I forget where I put the remote , or what I walked into the kitchen for. But I still remember every single note of that song. Like it's stitched into me.

"If only," I thought, staring into the cold dregs of my tea. "If only I could go back. Just for an hour. Just to do it properly."

Not as the clueless young lad I was. Not as the kid who thought buying a girl a warm bottle of Ritz made you boyfriend material. But as me , the man I am now.

The man who knows a little about how rare moments like that are, and how easy they are to waste. The man who's lived a little. Gotten things wrong. Learned a few things , some the hard way. But if I ever got the chance to go back, it wouldn't be as that clueless teenager who thought he knew it all. No , I'd want to go back with everything I know now. All the scars, the wisdom, the quiet regrets.

I said it out loud without even thinking: "I'd give anything for one more shot at it."

And in that moment, I didn't travel back. Not really. But I closed my eyes , and there I was. Young again. Stupid again. Heart racing like it used to. I could feel the sticky floor of the Galaxy Club under my feet, hear the music starting to swell. I knew it was all in my head , I did , but Jesus, it felt real.

One minute I was sitting there minding my own business, and the next I was 21 again, underdressed, overconfident, and heading straight for regret.

And me , somehow , standing there in my old leather jacket, my hair not yet gone thin at the crown, my hands young and unscarred.

"Funny thing is, I'm not even sure how I got here again. Not just tonight , I mean in general. But I know this place. Every inch of it, like it's tattooed somewhere deeper than memory."

I looked down at myself, blinking. Same battered trainers. Same battered dreams. But my mind , my heart , was the man I am now. All the knowledge. All the regrets. All the hopes. Folded into this younger body.

It should have been terrifying. Instead, it felt... right. Like putting on an old jacket and finding a fiver in the pocket.

At first, I thought, This has to be a dream. Some fever dream brought on by bad takeaway and bad memories. But when I brushed my hand against the rough texture of the brick wall, it felt real. When the heat of the crowd pressed against me, it felt real. When I caught the unmistakable scent of chip fat, stale smoke, and cheap perfume, it felt too bloody real.

I swallowed hard. Madonna's voice drifted out from the speakers, "I'm crazy for you..."

I turned my head , heart hammering against my ribs , and there she was.

She stood by the edge of the dancefloor, laughing with her friends, head thrown back, her hair catching the spinning lights. Not looking at me , not yet. But waiting. Somehow... waiting. I knew it in my bones. And this time , This time, I wasn't going to wait until the last bloody song.

I crossed the floor with the confidence of a man twice my age. Full of memories, regrets, and the odd decent haircut. And I asked her. Right there. Right then. At the very first bar of Madonna's "Crazy for You."

She looked at me, surprised but smiling. And she said yes.

We danced. Not the nervous shuffle I'd managed the first time around , all stiff arms and sweaty palms. This was smoother. Closer. Easy. She smiled like she'd been waiting for me to remember. And maybe she had.

Nothing more came of it. I wasn't trying to change history. She was still out of my league , or so I thought. I was still just a lad. An apprentice worker. No money. No grand plans. Just daydreams and the vague hope that the lotto might someday sort me out. We all thought that didn't we?

Anyhow, those things are worth going back for in my opinion. Not to change your life. Just to live the moment properly. To be present, even for a little while.

I remembered then , the rule I'd felt somewhere deep down , you can only go back once. No do overs. No rewinds.

And do you know what? That's more than enough.

Because the first time around, I waited until the final song of the slow set , George Michael's "Careless Whisper." That was the moment I finally leaned in for a kiss. Only to learn later, from her mate, that she would've kissed me from the very first bar of it.

You live and learn, don't you? And if you're lucky , just once , if the rain's right, and the wind blows in the right direction , you get the chance to go back and get it right.

I never did win the jackpot. But maybe that night… that moment… was my real win.

Chapter 2 : The Only Way Is Up

I must've drifted off humming Madonna, because when I opened my eyes, I could swear I was still there back in the Galaxy Club.

The lights, the smell, the music ,all of it just as it was. So real I could feel the bass in my chest.

For a second just a second I thought, here we go again. But then something shifted. I wasn't sure if I was dreaming, remembering, or slipping into something in between.

Maybe that's how it is when your head's full of old songs and long nights. Maybe the past doesn't stay where you left it. Maybe it waits for you, just behind your eyelids.

Either way, I stood there again or thought I did soaking it all in, just in case it slipped away again.

No panic. No rush. Just taking it all in. This wasn't a rerun. It wasn't even a memory I'd known I'd kept. The club had pulled back a different curtain , one I didn't know needed opening.

That same smell hit me , a mix of stale beer, cigarette smoke, and the finest selection of high street aftershave money could buy. It didn't even feel odd now. It felt normal, familiar, like I belonged here more than I ever did back in the day.

Yazz was already blasting from the speakers. "The Only Way is Up." Jesus, that tune could've raised the roof. The whole place bouncing, fists in the air, lads spilling pints, girls screaming the lyrics with absolute belief. We all believed it back then. That things were just about to kick off. That life was waiting, better and bigger, just round the corner if we could only hang in there long enough. "The only way is up, baby…" We needed to believe it. And for those three minutes, we did.

The club was still the place to be seen. Back in the day, it was where everything happened , romances started and ended, fights nearly kicked off and were mostly diffused by a mate holding your collar and going, "Leave it, he's not worth it." Girls got in for free before eleven if I remember right, while us eejits paid on the door and then paid again to hang our jackets up. Always thought that was a scam. We'd line up like sheep, wallets out, while the girls floated by, laughing and stamping their wrists like VIPs. Still stung even now.

And then there was the tech. The dancefloor would clear halfway through the night, and bang , down came the disco ball from the ceiling, lasers slicing through the smoke machine fog like something from Star Wars. At the time it felt totally futuristic, like we were stepping into tomorrow. The place would go quiet for a second, like everyone was holding their breath, and then the lights would explode , green, purple, blue , bouncing off the walls and faces, making everyone look ten times cooler than they really were. It was pure magic. For those moments, we all looked like pop stars.

I wandered over to the edge of the floor, keeping out of the way. It was all still going, still alive , the jeans, the shirts tucked in with way too much confidence, the hair sprayed into submission. And the heat , that proper club heat that stuck to you like a second skin. I could see versions of us everywhere. Posing. Lurking. Eyeing up the next move. Trying to be the lad who gets the nod before the slow set kicked in.

Then my stomach rumbled, and like a switch had been flipped, I remembered the food. The infamous curry. As part of the late night licensing laws, they had to serve what they called "substantial food" around midnight to justify flogging drink past closing. Substantial my arse , it was a lukewarm curry doled out on paper plates with plastic forks that bent if you looked at them funny. You needed your entry voucher to claim it, like some kind of golden ticket . Half the time you'd already lost it or it was in your mate's back pocket, covered in beer.

And yet we queued. We'd line up like it was a Michelin star meal, balancing our pints, pretending not to be that hungry. Then came the reality , you'd get your plate, take two steps, and boom , curry down your shirt. The same shirt your mam had ironed earlier with a bit of pride. A bit more would end up on your shoes, the rest smeared across your chin when you tried to eat while talking to a mate. You'd wipe your mouth with your hand, forget, and then go around all night with a curry fingerprint on your cheek. Then , and this was the best part , you'd stroll over to a girl, full of Dutch courage, thinking you looked a million dollars. Meanwhile, in reality, you had food on your collar, beer on your breath, and pupils the size of saucers. And somehow, you'd be confused when she said no , to the request to dance . Because in your head, you still looked like the lad you caught a glimpse of in the hallway mirror before you left the house , slick, sharp, invincible. We all did. And we were all deluded. But in the best, most beautiful way.

"I can still smell that cheap club curry if I think hard enough , mad how you forget what you had for breakfast, but you remember the taste of a dodgy vindaloo from 1989."

Anyhow I made my way toward the toilets, weaving through the crowd, still humming Yazz to myself. Then, as if on cue, the music shifted. Viola Wills. "Gonna Get Along Without You Now." Now there was a tune. A proper loo break anthem. The kind of song everyone knew the words to, whether they admitted it or not. As soon as it kicked in , "Ah,ha, woo,hoo, I'm gonna get along without you now…" , the whole place lit up. Even the fellas having a breather by the wall were mouthing along.

The toilets hadn't changed one bit. Same tiles, same dodgy taps, and , of course , the bathroom butler.

The poor lad in the tuxedo, standing stiff by the sinks, a tray of smelly sprays and breath mints laid out in front of him like sacred offerings. Nodding solemnly as you finished your business, motioning toward the Lynx can with all the ceremony of a priest offering communion. You'd wash your hands under freezing water, check yourself out in the cracked mirror , shirt ruined, curry round your mouth, pupils like dinner plates , and before you could escape, he'd squirt a mist of Lynx and gesture meaningfully toward the overflowing tip ashtray.

Not a full spray, mind you.
A squirt.
Half a squirt, if you were unlucky.

The fella would have about twenty different bottles after a few years , Davidoff, Joop, Fahrenheit , probably worth a fortune if you added it all up.

And somehow, somehow, it became a thing.
A proper job.

I stared at myself for a bit. Longer than I meant to. I didn't look younger this time. Not like before. I looked like… me. Now. But something inside felt lighter. Like I was carrying less. Like I'd finally let go of whatever I'd dragged in here the first time. She wasn't here , and I didn't expect her to be anymore. That hope had passed. But it didn't hurt, not like it did. This place , the noise, the nonsense, the magic , it had done something. Healed something. Quietly. In the background.

I nodded to the bathroom butler, dropped in a few coins, and walked out. The music was rising again, another tune kicking off, the crowd screaming like it was their national anthem. And for a second, I just stood there. Took it all in. The lights, the sound, the madness of it all. It wasn't about reliving it exactly , it was about remembering how it felt. How alive it was. And how lucky I'd been to be part of it, even in my curry stained shirt and busted shoes.

One night. One memory. That's all you get.

Or maybe not.

Maybe your mind finds ways to sneak back in when you're not looking. Just for a while.

Chapter 3: Two Tribes

Like all the places to go out to at the weekend, the spots changed over time. Some were new, some old, some we never got into, and some we never wanted to return to. Most of the time, we'd find new pubs with new girls, thanks to one of the lads who was an apprentice barman in one of the city centre hotels. He knew all the other apprentice barmen around town, because they all attended barman school/college. (Believe it or not, that was a thing back then. Lads would serve an apprenticeship as a barman, becoming an expert in all things beer, wine, spirits, and hospitality.) It doesn't happen anymore, but you could walk into any pub in the world, and you'd know a lad who was a "real barman," someone who'd served his time. He could pull any pint, serve a crowd of customers at once, and still manage to chat and be friendly. Unlike the lads behind the bar today, most of whom couldn't pull a pint if their life depended on it.

Anyway, he knew all the lads who worked in the new trendy places and could often get us in, skipping the queues and making the whole night feel like we knew exactly what we were doing. More often than not, we'd stroll up to the door, past the queues, and walk straight in after the bouncers recognized our mate. Simple as that.

But sometimes, he'd have to work, and we'd be left queuing ourselves. Every night wasn't successful in gaining entry, but most of the time, we knew that if we couldn't get in here, we'd get in somewhere else. Lucky, I suppose, that we managed to manoeuvre around the city's nightspots like we were seasoned pros. In the end, someone always knew someone who'd get us into the local, trendy spots.

As the years went on, though, we each found our own favourite spots. The truth was, we didn't care about the exclusive clubs or the latest must visit places. What we wanted was to spend our nights out with the same group of friends, because, as a rule, we had great craic and the same sense of fun and humour. We'd enjoy ourselves wherever we went.

Funny how some nights come back clearer than the day I'm in. I can't remember what I had for lunch yesterday, but I remember exactly how it felt to walk past that queue like we owned the place. Sometimes I wonder if I'm remembering it or just inside it again.

One night, we swanned up to this new bar. One of the lads had heard, through a friend of a friend, that this was the "new place to be seen." The long queues told us everything we needed to know about how busy it was, so we joined in and waited our turn, as usual. Of course, as per usual, a group of pretty girls would rock up, give the ugly looking bouncers a little wink, and be let straight in. The bouncers, believing they might just get a kiss and a cuddle later if they were lucky, let them skip the line. (Not that this was ever the reality, but we all liked to think it was.) But as lads, we were always left outside, made to feel like criminals.

Eventually, it was our turn. There were six or seven of us, and the bouncer at the front was usually the loud one the one with the big mouth who liked to give it large. You know the type: Billy Big Balls with his muscle lads standing by, ready in case anyone decided to push back.

"Evening, lads. Where are you coming from?"

We'd learned the hard way not to mention certain areas. You know, the places where we lived, just in case it didn't fit the image they were looking for. We had to look like well groomed, nice young men, so we made sure to play the part. Zero reason to turn us away, but some idiot always found an excuse.

Some of the excuses were ridiculous. "Your face doesn't fit," or "There's already too many lads inside; we need more girls in here." But no, the bouncer would find something ridiculous to refuse us entry.

The golden rule most nights was: either we all went in, or none of us did. And most bouncers knew that. What friend would leave a mate outside while they went in to enjoy themselves? Sure, we'd all done it occasionally, but that was usually when drink was involved, or there was a girl involved but normally, we stuck together.

The excuses were endless: "No jeans." "White socks!" "No runners." "Your hair's too short." "Your hair's too long." "You've got earrings." "No skinny leather ties." "No side laced shoes." (Believe it or not, that was a massive thing in the '80s, I kid you not.) "No ID," and so on. The list just went on and on.

So, there we were, standing out in the cold far too long, having had a few cans earlier to get a bit of a buzz going. No money, so we couldn't afford the full night out. We'd started a little earlier in the park, behind the swimming pool, or at someone's house while the parents were out shopping on a Friday after tea time. Or they'd gone to Mass on Saturday night, so we had the "free gaff" for a bit of drinking before heading out.

(They had gone to mass on a Saturday evening as they wouldn't be arsed getting up on a Sunday to go. That was a thing you know, Sunday mass on Saturday, I kid you not, probably the start of the fall of mass going for many of us. Anyhow, the free gaff, as we called it, would contribute to the early drinking.)

Anyhow, to cut a long story short, we needed a slash, a toilet break. So, we wandered down the lane, far enough that no one would see us. No butler standing around with a tissue or a spray of Lynx, I'm afraid. Just a bunch of lads needing to go.

And down that dark laneway, of course, was a door. A door no one would know about. It was open when,somehow,someone pushed it. And there we were,da dah!,the backdoor to the bar we'd just been refused entry to.

"Thank you very much," we said to the door, and just like that, we were inside

The bouncers were too busy to even notice us, and we quickly moved through the crowd, away from the slow set playing on the speakers . "Lady in Red" , a sigh and a tut followed , no way were we hanging around for that. As soon as we could, we found a spot by the bar, soaking in the moment.

Just as we were standing there, feeling like we had pulled off the greatest heist of all time, the DJ dropped Frankie Goes to Hollywood's "Two Tribes," and the place instantly exploded with energy. The bass thudded through the speakers, and the crowd went wild. It wasn't the Lady in Red slow jam we had walked in on, but it was the perfect pick-me-up. We stood there, grinning like idiots, as the vibe turned electric around us. There we were, surrounded by sweaty bodies, feeling like we were part of something big, something we weren't even supposed to be a part of.

We hadn't spent a penny on the entry. We weren't even supposed to be there. But somehow, we were.

But the challenges had only begun .

The delicate balance of dancing without spilling your pint all over yourself or someone else. Spilling drinks onto the floor , glasses smashing ,turning the place into a skating rink , one misstep and you'd be on your arse .The challenges a night out can bring .

And as I stood there, thinking about the whole night, it hit me. Memories are funny that way. I lose track of my keys all the time, but that night? I remember it like it was last night. Sometimes, what we think we want isn't exactly what we end up enjoying. The queue, the refusal, the sneaky backdoor entrance, it all made the night something much more memorable than just another night in a club.

It wasn't about getting in; it was about the craic along the way. And when you're young, the craic is everything. Sometimes I wonder why these old nights come back so sharp, like they're queuing up for one last spin while the rest of my memories fade to static.

Funny how some of our best moments come from getting told 'no.'

Chapter 4 : Too Shy

Reliving those old nights out still gives me a buzz , not like watching a video, but like stepping inside a moment that never really left me. Some memories just don't fade. They play in the background of your mind, ready to flicker to life when the right song comes on.

I never go back to the exact same night, not really , just bits of them. Flashes. Feelings. Faces that meant everything for five minutes. And still do, some days.

But still, I soaked it in, casually observing everything around me with that mix of familiarity and awe.

Then there were the dancefloor politics , the slow set moments .You'd be dancing near someone, hovering, waiting , sure the DJ would hit us with a slow number soon. You could always tell when it was coming too. He'd bait the floor with a girlie anthem , maybe Cyndi Lauper's "Girls Just Want to Have Fun" or "It's Raining Men" by The Weather Girls , the kind of tunes that packed the floor with women dancing in circles, girl power before it was a thing, sometimes literally dancing around their handbags like they were guarding treasure.

I don't know why these nights play out so vividly. It's like I'm not just remembering them , I'm there, hovering by the edge, hoping for the nod. Maybe my head's got its own jukebox, and every now and then it drops a track I thought I'd forgotten.

That circle was nearly impossible to break unless you'd already been given the nod.

Us lads would sort of shuffle around the edges, pretending not to care, casually positioning ourselves near someone you liked the look of , watching, hoping, plotting. You knew it was coming. Then boom , the unmistakable first bars of Peter Cetera's "Glory of Love", the theme from The Karate Kid. That was your cue.

And just like that, we'd all move forward like half cut karate kids, all trying to reach a girl who caught our eye, quicker than Mr. Miyagi could say "wax on, wax off" , before some other muppet got in there first.

You'd lock eyes , maybe , then both look away like it never happened, only to try again a few minutes later, just to see her dancing with someone else. That was the game. Sometimes it worked, often it didn't.

And then the worst of it , asking her to dance in front of her mates, only to get the head shake and polite smile that said, "No Thanks." And off you went, the walk of shame back through the crowd, pretending you were just heading to the jacks anyway. Smooth ,the heartbreak shuffle.

Sometimes you'd just stand there, watching the crowd , taking it all in. There was always a few characters that stood out.

Like the sweaty guy who took it way too seriously. You know the type , thought he was in a music video, sunglasses on indoors, arms flailing everywhere, knocking over people's drinks like he was trying to swat flies. Completely lost in the music… but not in a good way.

Then you had the lads dragged along against their will. The reluctant wingmen. They never left the edge of the dancefloor, just stood there awkwardly all night, arms folded or hands in pockets, tapping one foot now and then like it was their first time hearing a beat.

And then, of course, there was the Dancefloor DJ.

We've all been him at some point (well, I definitely have). Propping up the side of the booth, drink in hand, shouting over the music, pleading with the actual DJ to throw on a bit of Kajagoogoo or Duran Duran , as if that one track was going to change the course of the entire night.

And then there was the end of, the night cloakroom queues , Jesus, they were chaos. You'd try and grab someone's number, all charming and confident, only to come back after waiting half an hour for your coat and find they'd vanished. Probably didn't even give you their real name. Half the time, the gobshites in front had lost their tickets, holding up the whole line while the staff rummaged through 300 black puffa jackets that all looked the same.

Years later came the smoking ban, and mad as it sounds, it actually improved your odds. People bonded out in the rain, under smoking shelter awnings, shivering but talking shite between drags. Many a romance lit up over a borrowed lighter or a shared notion about the weather.

Since we only lived a couple of miles from the city centre, walking home was usually the norm. God knows how we got away with it , never got hassled, never ran into trouble. Just lucky, I suppose. Then again, we weren't the type to go looking for it either. But now and then, when the feet were sore or the rain was biblical, you'd treat yourself to a taxi.

Queue up with the late night herd, sobering up in the cold. Taxi drivers never hid their annoyance when they heard where you were going , "Down the road? That's it?" , raging that they wouldn't be getting a proper fare out of you. But it was worth it, just to not arrive home soaked or frozen.

Other times, you'd share a taxi with random strangers, usually heading to an afterparty you'd just heard about on the way out the door. Gatecrashing was part of the culture. Half the time, the "party" never existed, or had already fizzled out , and you'd be facing a long bloody walk home from some estate you didn't even recognise.

Still, some of those parties... if only I could remember half of them as well as the other lads. Gold dust, those memories , even the blurry ones.

Chapter 5 : DeDoDoDo DeDaDaDa

Music had always been a major part of my life, even though I never played any instruments. It was the one thing that could take me back to a place or time, like a soundtrack to my memories. You know, the kind of music that doesn't just fill the silence, but fills your soul, instantly transporting you somewhere else , somewhere better.

One of fondest music memory, though, takes me back to the summer of 1985. Live Aid. That iconic concert, that was my moment. Even though I knew I couldn't stay in that moment forever , that was the rule, right? One night, one last look, then back to reality.

But before Live Aid, like most houses, Thursday night TV meant one thing: Top of the Pops. A mere 30 minutes, but for us, it was the highlight of the week. Every Thursday , glued around the telly ,The top DJs of the day would introduce the bands and tell the public which songs topped the charts that week. It wasn't just about the music; it was about the stories behind the songs, the buzz of what was coming next.

Tomorrows World (the TV show) used to be on just before Top of the Pops. Most people only remember the last five minutes of it , we'd only watch in case we missed the start of TOTP. But it was all about the future, about the technologies that would one day become part of everyday life. Stuff you couldn't even understand properly at the time, but still thought looked cool. Things like digital watches, mobile phones, Walkman, CD players, camcorders...

But my personal favourite was the night they showed a television being mounted on a big shelf on a wall, and said this would become common practice in every household.
I laughed out loud at that one. In our house, the height of technology was the tape recorder.

Now, I'd sit in front of the telly with my tape recorder, waiting for Top of the Pops to start. And if there was even a hint of a new song or one of my favourites, I'd jump into action , pressing "play" and "record" at the same time to capture it.
Silence was absolutely vital during this ritual.

More often than not, though, someone would ruin it. A cough. A door slamming. A voice shouting, "What's this shite?" right in the middle of the recording.

Strangely, I also remember being forced to stay quiet when one of Mam or Dad's favourites came on. Mam loved bloody Cliff Richard , he was always on and never seemed to age. Dad liked Tom Jones, who'd

appear now and again, but he had a real soft spot for ABBA.
I realise now he was probably more taken with the blonde one than the band.

As a teenager, you were practically required to hate your parents' music. But that changed the day I was finally allowed to use the record player. That was a whole new world , raiding Dad's record collection and discovering sounds I'd never heard before. That's where I found The Beatles, The Monkees, The Everly Brothers , all the bands seemed to be called "The" something or other.

Which brings me back to another moment, burned into my memory.

I was in front of the telly one Saturday morning, tape recorder in hand, fully prepped. I'd been watching Swap Shop all morning, waiting for the promised exclusive first showing of the new song by The Police , my favourite band at the time. The song? "De Do Do Do, De Da Da Da."

Picture the scene: I'm standing there, heart racing, finger over the record button, the most important moment of my young life about to unfold...

And then Mam strolls into the room, hoover in hand , just as the song starts.

She unplugs the TV.
Plugs in the hoover.

Totally unaware that my world had just crashed down around me.

She gives me that look , the one that says, "You've been watching TV long enough, I'm only plugging it out for a few minutes , you can watch it after."

Watch it after? Watch what?

It won't be De Do Do Do, De Da Da Da, I can tell you that.

Now, Dad had a record player , well, technically it was a three in one stereo system: radio, record player, and tape recorder all in one. A total game changer. You could record songs off the radio without unwanted background noise and even copy entire albums onto cassette. Piracy of sorts, really , you'd just borrow an album off a mate and record it instead of buying your own copy.

Most of the albums I had were ones I'd asked for as presents , birthdays, Christmas, that sort of thing. Being the eldest child, I didn't have an older sibling's music collection to raid, so my own piracy mainly came from friends or the radio.

Now, recording off the radio became a skill you honed over time , pausing the tape just before the DJ started yapping, getting the timing just right so your mix tape sounded as close as possible to a proper greatest hits album from the shops. It was an art form. A rite of passage.

Now, my mix tapes before Live Aid were a collection of songs from albums I actually owned. An odd range of tastes, maybe , but brilliant in their own way. I played them over and over again, and even now, rediscovering those tracks brings me straight back every time.

Adam and the Ants – Prince Charming, The Police – Zenyatta Mondatta, Madness – Madness 7, and Kajagoogoo – White Feathers. They were mine. And sure, I know they're not everyone's cup of tea, but I loved them all. At different times, they each made perfect sense in my pre-teen world.

Then came Now That's What I Call Music , the first compilation album packed with all the hit songs of the day. That series became a massive success, and it's still going strong today. I remember that first album vividly , Kajagoogoo had not one but two tracks on it, and Madness featured as well. Great times.

Chapter 6 : Bohemian Rhapsody

Then came the summer of '85. Live Aid. And everything changed. My dad had made sure we had enough blank cassette tapes ready to go, so I could record whatever I wanted. The concert was being broadcast on both radio and TV at the same time, which meant I could get a clean recording , no background noise, no slamming doors, no one shouting over it. Just pure music.

Basically, this was going to be a concert featuring everyone from Top of the Pops , performing live. Every artist singing their biggest hits. We were told we were in for a treat, and for once, they weren't exaggerating.

Now, I don't believe for one second that anyone who bought tickets thought it was going to be that big of a deal. And I honestly don't know a single person who wouldn't have loved to have been there.

The concert was held at Wembley Stadium. The only time I'd seen Wembley on TV before that was for the FA Cup Final , but this time, the pitch was packed with people, music lovers crammed shoulder to shoulder. The stage was set up behind one of the goals and looked absolutely massive. When it appeared on screen, I was blown away.

I used my loaf, as they say, turned the volume down on the TV and turned the stereo on. We had two speakers, so it made sense. Like we were having our own little gig in the living room.

Funny thing is, I can't remember anyone else being in the room, or maybe it just felt like no one else was. Like the music built a little world around me for the day. I was so completely absorbed. Everything felt surreal, but it was all really happening. The line, up was a who's who of the music world. Not only was there a gig happening in England, but another one was set to kick off in the USA later, with even more superstars. And all of it was being broadcast live, right into our sitting room.

My blank cassette was loaded, and I was ready for the first band. I had no idea who it would be. Turned out, it was one of my dad's favourites, Status Quo. Their anthem "Rockin' All Over the World" kicked things off. It was the perfect start to what became a watershed moment, when music became a force for change, a kind of revolution.

Adam Ant came on soon after, I was delighted. Then more familiar faces from Top of the Pops rolled out one after another, performing their hits in the sunshine. It was perfect.

The TV stayed on in the background all day, as I drifted in and out of the kitchen for ham and cheese sandwiches and endless pots of tea. Record, record, record. Not everything, but the stuff I liked , Nick Kershaw, Howard Jones, Sting (without The Police), Paul Young, Alison Moyet. The gig was properly underway.

I had to flip the cassette to Side B just in time for the next act , an Irish band called U2. I was ready to record everything they said, just in case they gave a shout out to Dublin or something. On they came: "Sunday Bloody Sunday." I knew that one. Most bands were given about three songs or a twenty minute slot , I can't quite remember. Then another song started , 'Bad.' I'd never heard of it, to be honest. But the next fifteen minutes would change everything.

That performance introduced U2 to the world in a way they couldn't have dreamed of. They were electric , not my favourite band by any means , but they delivered something different. Bono jumped off the stage mid song, pulled a couple of girls from the crowd, gave them a hug, overwhelmed by the moment. Meanwhile, the band just kept the song going, letting it build.

For those few minutes, Bono wasn't just a singer , he became the showman of Wembley. It was mesmerising.

Bryan Adams took to the stage next from the USA, followed by The Beach Boys , legends in their own right. Then it was back to Wembley, and this time, for Queen.

Now, I'll be honest , I was never really into Queen. But that Freddie Mercury lad… Jesus. I thought Bono was good, but Freddie? He had the whole world eating from the palm of his hand by the time he hit "We Are the Champions."

He'd already led the entire crowd , all 72,000 of them , in a full, on singalong to "Bohemian Rhapsody." And during "Radio Ga Ga," they were clapping in perfect unison, like something out of a film. It was breathtaking to watch. Everyone at home, me included, wishing more than anything that we were there.

It was one of those rare moments you could feel, even though the screen. Something bigger than the songs, bigger than the concert. Freddie wasn't just performing , he was commanding the moment.

I only really came around to appreciating Queen properly years later, unfortunately around the time Freddie Mercury passed away. But that performance planted the seed. It stayed with me.

By now, the blank cassette tapes were being filled and recorded over at speed. So much happening, so fast , I couldn't capture it all, but I did my best.

Millions of people around the world tuned in to watch the concert. Live Aid wasn't just a music event , it was a global phenomenon. A massive benefit concert organised to raise awareness and funds for the devastating famine in Ethiopia, caused by drought and civil war. It changed music history and redefined what global philanthropy could look like.

The concert rolled on late into the night, and I have vivid memories of acts like David Bowie performing "Heroes". He'd originally planned a cross continent duet with Mick Jagger, but they settled instead on a pre-recorded video of "Dancing in the Street". Still, it was electric.

And then there was Bob Geldof, the driving force behind it all, losing the plot live on TV, shouting, "Give us the fucking money!" down the camera. You didn't forget that kind of moment , raw, desperate, real.

One of the most iconic stunts of the day was Phil Collins. He performed with Sting at Wembley in the afternoon, then jumped on Concorde to fly to the U.S. so he could play drums with the legendary Led Zeppelin that evening. It was madness , and brilliance.

That day, I got a real education in music. Not just the sounds, but the power it holds. How it can bring people together, raise voices, open hearts , and maybe, just maybe, change the world.

Funny how some days blur together, but that one? That one stayed sharp. Stayed bright. For a long time, anyway.

Chapter 7 : Pretty in Pink

I was watching some old movie the other night on one of the satellite channels. I can't remember what it was called, but nowadays movies or films, as we call them, are available whenever you want to watch them.

I remember the only movies you'd see were at Christmas time on the telly, the big blockbusters that would've been in the cinema a few years before. The latest James Bond or something similar.

Which reminds me, remember when you'd have to queue outside the cinema on the footpath with everyone else, waiting your turn to get inside? Being greeted by a lad dressed in a suit with a bow tie, like he was going to a wedding?

Well, I remember my dad bringing me to see the latest James Bond, only to be told at the door that I was underage and Bond would've been unsuitable for a young lad, too much violence, adult humour, all that, which would've definitely gone over my head. But anyhow, we couldn't go in.

But you see, we'd already bought our drinks and our bon bons, so we weren't going bloody home.

The usher lad suggested we go into a space movie, as he described it, hinting that all the kids loved it. "That'll do," as they say. So in we went.

Shown to our seats, lights went out, movie started.

"A long time ago in a galaxy far, far away..."

And that was me. I had found my people. My genre. Science fiction it was to be.

I loved everything about science fiction movies. Still do today. Pure escapism.

Anyhow, we were lucky enough to see another Tomorrow's World prediction come true when we were introduced to VHS videos and tapes.

Films became available to watch on your TV, you just plugged this player into the back of the telly, and the tapes, instead of music on them, had movies. The ones you'd normally wait years to see on the telly were now available to watch in your own house.

Your own home cinema, they called it.

Now, not everyone could afford such a luxury, but you'd always know someone's family that had one, so you'd be asked around to watch the latest Jaws or Indiana Jones or whatever was available in the video shop.

Yes, a shop with all the bloody movies you could think of. Like a library, but without the books. A great place to be seen for any young film buff.

As the summer holidays provided a lot of time off, you'd watch loads of movies you definitely wouldn't have seen in the actual cinema. All the classics, like The Breakfast Club, Pretty in Pink, Psychedelic Furs "Pretty in Pink" – great tune , great band, Back to the Future, Highlander, Terminator , E.T , Top Gun ,we were spoiled. Dead Poet Society "Captain my captain" and "carpe diem" bloody brilliant .

Now and again someone would get an over,18s movie like Porky's or Platoon, but I'll always remember the day we got to see The Life of Brian. Absolutely brilliant.

A comedy version of everything you'd ever heard in Mass on a Sunday. Absolutely brilliant, blasphemy at its best.

It was banned in Ireland, but somehow... we got a copy.

Now, while we were able to watch movies , the TV sets were a lot smaller than the big ones we have today, maybe 20 inches in size if you were lucky. None of these 36,inch flat screens.

But Jesus, they weighed a ton, with that big square back on them full of bulbs and wires.

They'd break down from time to time.

You'd need to call out the TV repair man if the rabbit ears on top of the telly didn't get a reception, or if, after banging the shit out of the side of it trying to get the picture perfect, it still wouldn't work. The picture flickered, like my thoughts these days, half-there, half-not.

Now, when he called to fix it, usually on a Saturday in our house, I'd sit there praying he'd have to take it away to fix in his workshop.

Because if he did, you see, he'd leave you a replacement set, which was usually the latest model.

Now, it might just have square buttons instead of round ones, but sometimes it had six buttons instead of four, which meant, on a sunny day, you'd be able to tune in HTV from Wales.

I can't recall exactly why we liked to watch it, but I do remember it being popular in our house.

I remember having mostly just RTÉ and RTÉ2 to watch stuff. BBC1 and BBC2 as well.

Mam and Dad would watch RTÉ for the news, The Late Late Show, and horse jumping, stuff like that.

We'd watch the BBC, especially in the mornings, Saturday mornings, for the latest shows like Hong Kong Phooey or The Banana Splits (still the best theme tune ever!). Then there was Swap Shop and later Saturday Superstore, where you'd get your weekend fix of music videos and pop star studio guests.

BBC2 never had much going on, unless you were into watching dogs chasing sheep around a field, listening to a farmer blowing a bloody whistle in his mouth. I kid you not, this was actually a TV show.

RTÉ ruled the airwaves until Channel 4 sneaked into our lives and changed Irish TV choices forever.

Channel 4 was a huge upgrade. Its risqué content, like Eurotrash or the music programme The Tube, and those late, night movies felt like a rebellious act against the Irish station.

Father Ted would become a huge hit with Irish viewers years later, despite being on an English channel, after RTÉ had turned it down, saying nobody would be interested in that type of comedy.

"Down with that sort of thing."

"...and yet, no matter how many channels we had, I'd still drift back to that first time in the cinema. Me, Dad, a bag of bon bons, and a galaxy far, far away. I think I've been chasing that feeling ever since."

Chapter 8 : Last Christmas

You know that smell, cinnamon, gingerbread, pine trees. Well, pine tree scented spray in our case. We never had a real tree, not at home anyway. Always an artificial one. Handy to store in the attic along with the box of baubles and lights. But still, that Christmas smell. That's the one that always brings me back. My favourite time of year.

Christmas can, and always will, bring me back. I could return for many one-last-looks.

Everything about it stuck with me.

The telly at Christmas? You didn't really need a TV guide, though there was usually a fifty page pullout in one of the papers that became your bible for the two week holidays, especially as a kid.

Classic ads like the Coke-Cola ("Holidays are coming…"), the Guinness ad , you know the one when it snows and yer man says "Don't forget to turn the lights off" and Pennys "Penny got a lot of things for Christmas" , Jesus ,the things you remember.

Willy Wonka, Chitty Chitty Bang Bang for us little ones. And The Sound of Music and The Great Escape for the parents, those were permanently cemented into the Christmas lineup, whether you wanted to watch them or not.

Christmas Day always had one proper highlight: the festive Top of the Pops. They had everyone, and I mean everyone who had a hit that year. Decked out in their silly jumpers, singing their songs. It always got the day off to a cracking start.

Music at Christmas was always great. Some call it tacky, others call it festive but most of those songs are now considered classics. They're still played and sung, all over the world every December.

In the '80s, we were lucky enough to hear them the first time around. And we still hear them today: Wham's "Last Christmas," Mariah Carey's "All I Want for Christmas," Chris Rea's "Driving Home for Christmas," The Pogues and Kirsty MacColl's "Fairytale of New York", just to name a few.

The Christmas number one single was one of the highlights of the year. Every band wanted that honour. It doesn't seem to carry the same weight anymore, but back then, it was massive.

Now, the Christmas tree debate, real or fake? We were an artificial tree family. Still are. Crowned with the same old star, bent at the top from years of being shoved on. Some people put a fairy on top, but that was never us. Though I did stick a Darth Vader toy up there one year, with a bauble star hanging from his lightsabre. True story, I kid you not.

But the baubles, now they could tell stories. Cheap ones from Spain. A glass bell from Egypt. A slightly wonky Eiffel Tower from Paris. Nearly all our decorations were souvenirs from holidays, and every year, as we decorated the tree, we relived those memories.

Now, other decorations? They left a lot to be desired. Christ, we made some of them out of loo rolls. And if I remember rightly, crepe paper. Whatever that was.

Then there were the Christmas crackers, stuffed with absolute rubbish: fortune telling fish that curled in your palm, mini measuring tapes (like anyone needed another one), paper hats that split the second you put them on, and jokes so bad they were stupidly funny.

But my earliest memory?

Me and my sister heading upstairs on Christmas Eve, after leaving out the carrots and the drink for Santa. It was always the hardest night to fall asleep , afraid you'd getting nothing if you caught Santa , afraid he'd see you looking .

Stockings hanging on the bedroom door, that was the sign. If there was something in the stocking when you woke up (usually a bag of gold chocolate coins), it meant he'd been. That he'd checked you were asleep and delivered the right toys to the right house.

And if the stocking had something in it, no matter how small, that was the signal: time to run downstairs at some ungodly hour to see what was under the tree.

Hoping you got what was on your letter. Hoping maybe he'd seen something you'd circled in the toy store catalogue too.

We always got enough. Games like Kerplunk, Hungry Hippos, Operation and Cabbage Patch kids were big favourites and space hoppers ,how could we forget them . But, oddly enough, I always remember the annuals, The Dandy and Shoot!, being right at the top of my list.

There's always that one toy that you open with shaky excitement, only to find out it needs six AAA batteries. And guess what? Nowhere open on Christmas Day.

Santa never forgot. Well, almost never. But I'll tell you about that another time. When I recall it exactly.

Still... It never snows at Christmas the way Bing Crosby suggested it does, does it?

Chapter 9 : Alive and Kicking

Once I started earning a few quid, my mix tapes naturally got better or at least I thought they did. It was my taste after all, and looking back now, those tapes were basically the soundtrack of my life.

Most of the lads had a favourite band or genre. Some were into guitar bands like Oasis, Ocean Colour Scene, and later on, Snow Patrol, Keane, and The Killers. Others leaned more pop, A-ha, Wet Wet Wet, Bros, U2, Madness, Frankie Goes to Hollywood. Then there were the heavy metal lads. God love them. I still don't get it, just noise to me. I loved electronic music the most, it's still my go to. Music made mostly from electronic pianos, keyboards, and computers. Noise to some people, but Mozart to me. Pet Shop Boys , Depeche Mode all made sense to me .

One of the lads had only two albums: Simple Minds and, I swear to God, Nanci Griffith. But from a distance we were alive and kicking ! (See what I did there?)

I recall I worked in a record shop for a while, still the best job I ever had. Like a kid in a candy store. Imagine being allowed to play any song you wanted, all day, every day. That was me. And of course, I did my bit for home piracy, filling up blank cassette tapes weekly with whatever I fancied.

There were two main tape related nightmares back then. First, running out of blank cassettes. But my dad had a hack for that: stick a bit of Sellotape over the holes on top of a tape you didn't like anymore, and boom, you could record over it. The height of piracy in our house.

And then there was the other nightmare, the dreaded tape unravelling. Jesus, the brown ribbon would get loose, twist, and spool out like a scene from a horror movie. That's when you'd grab a Bic biro like it was Doctor Who's sonic screwdriver and start twisting it back into the cassette, one careful crank at a time. After what felt like 43 rotations, you'd finally pop it back in, hit play, and pray the song would still sound the same. It always did, of course because you, my friend, were the tech genius of the day.

Now, while I didn't have a ghetto blaster myself to parade around the streets, one of the lads always did, capable of blasting the latest mix tape out loud for all to hear. Most had just one tape deck, but a few had two, a double tape deck! That was like having your own outdoor DJ setup. We'd spend endless summer days lazing on the local green, listening to music. Everyone's music. Even Nancie.

The only heartbreak we understood back then? When your favourite tape got chewed up.

It's funny how precious a mix tape became. The thrill of making the perfect playlist . In fairness, only nightclub DJs had access to the records we all dreamed of, albums and singles ready to go at the drop of a needle. I was always a bit envious of the massive boxes they'd drag into the DJ booth like musical treasure chests. Years later, if you'd told me I'd have everything they had and more available in my pocket, on a phone, I'd have laughed you out of it. I'd have said you'd had one too many pints while watching Tomorrow's World to come out with something that outrageous.

Nothing worse than bringing your mix tape along to a party, waiting your turn to be DJ, and realising you brought the wrong tape. Cassettes always looked the same unless you labelled them with that little sticker that came inside the box, for that exact reason. You'd pop it in, only for Dolly Parton or Kenny Rogers to blast out of the speakers. Quickly realising your embarrassing mistake, you'd flip over to the B-side, praying the tape had some sort of credibility on the other side but usually, it was shite as well.

Embarrassed, you just shrugged your shoulders, blamed a family member for the disaster, and pretended someone else's mix tape was good enough to listen to either way. It wasn't though. It never was.

Always fancied the DJ thing. The idea of playing my kind of music out on the airwaves for lads to record for their own mix tapes at home really appealed. I blagged my way into various DJ boxes on the continent over the years on holidays, spun a few tracks, quickly got bored, and just wanted to dance to the music, not play it. Not really for me.

Now, the holidays they were always for me. Best days of my life, lads' holidays were. Great memories, if only I could remember half the craic we had. I could tell you stories, only I'd get into trouble and with all those holiday songs working like time machines , taking me back reminding me again .

But Jesus, we had a great time. We partied in all the best clubs, danced to all the best music or our kind of music, anyhow. Been there, as they say, and got the T-shirts to prove it.

Chapter 10 : Lady in Red

I was writing a letter the other day. Well, that's a lie, nobody writes letters these days. I was signing my name, probably signing my life away next to a big X on some form or other. But it took me back to when we used to write in school. You know that moment when you graduated from pencil to pen.

In our school, for a while at least, we used a thing called a fountain pen (Jesus, the things I remember). Now, the fountain pen was a bit more advanced than a quill (Google it if you must), but still pretty old-school. Ours was made of wood, with a metal nib you dipped into ink. The inkwell was built into the desk (go on, Google that too), and you'd dip the pen, write a letter or two, dip again, and keep going until you finished the word.

Why they made us use that instead of a good old Bic biro, I'll never know. You'd make a mess on the page half the time. Thankfully, we were allowed to use blotting paper (yep, that's another one for the search bar). The unsung hero of fountain pen users, a soft, blue sheet that quietly soaked up the excess ink and saved your page from smudges and puddles.

If you never used blotting paper, congratulations but you're probably either lying or the type who's moved on to using a Montblanc (go ahead, one more Google).

Eventually, after we'd mastered our ABCs and big words like Czechoslovakia (yet another relic, maybe even another search), they let us use fountain pens with ink cartridges. A step up in technology, sure but you still needed the blotting paper.

Now back in those days we did not have morning assemblies, you know the gatherings students have now where everyone meets for announcements and news before class starts or all that health and safety nonsense. You just ran around the school yard, fell, grazed your knees, got up and got on with it. You'd be back the next day with a patch over your knee or elbow, hiding where you'd ripped your uniform the day before. The whole school was full of patched up uniforms, no big deal, nobody cared. Simpler times.

Now and then you'd fall into nettles chasing a ball into the overgrown grass, or get stung by a bee or wasp. But you soldiered on. You'd grab a dock leaf, think that's what they were called, rub the sting, and just like magic, all would be cured. That, or a spoon of Milk of Magnesia your mam would give you. That white, milky, blue bottle she kept in the press, the chalky one with the dried bits around the cap. It cured every ailment. Well, it did in our house.

As I remember we didn't have assembly, but we did have morning prayers. They bellowed out of the speakers at 9 a.m. sharp, and everyone stood to attention beside their desks, like what I imagine a military school might've looked like. The Hail Mary, the Our Father, and the Glory Be were blasted from the speakers while we mumbled along, half hoping the teacher wouldn't catch you rolling your eyes or smirking at the ritual. It was a daily punishment, or, I mean, a daily tradition that somehow got us through to the bell.

In a weird way, it worked. Well, at the very least, it knocked five minutes off the lesson.

Back to the writing thing. After the fountain pen debacle, the teachers thought it might be a good idea to practice writing letters. Now, of course, there was a catch, there always was in school. The catch here? You had to practice writing letters and actually send them to somebody. But not to anyone you knew, no family members or friends could avail themselves of our writing skills. This honour was reserved for a pen pal.

Let me explain that phenomenon to you. You'd write to a pen pal agency, stating you wanted to correspond with someone abroad who shared similar interests, ideally someone your age but foreign, who didn't have a clue who you were. The idea was to become sort, of friends. I had two such pals for a few years, but eventually, the letters just stopped, whether from my end or theirs, I can't recall.

What I do remember, oddly enough, are their names: Anna from Poland and Christian from Denmark.

The letters were mostly about school, favourite bands, football teams, hobbies, and so on. We'd exchange posters, pages torn from Smash Hits or similar magazines and stamps from our countries.

Stamp collecting was a big hobby for kids back then, alongside coins. Stamps were my thing. I always assumed I'd eventually swap an old Irish stamp for a Penny Black, the holy grail of philately. Surely it'd turn up in a swap someday!

Coins were another treasure: pesetas from Spain, lira from Italy, francs from France, and the coveted American dollar. Everyone collected something.

Anna was from Poland, great stamps, but mix tapes were a no go. I'd send them over, but they always got intercepted entering Eastern Europe. We were basically trying to smuggle contraband. Once, she asked for a Chris de Burgh tape. It never arrived. She wrote back saying the letter came in a big brown envelope, but the cassette was missing.

It wasn't that Top of the Pops was banned there; they just didn't have access to "our" stuff beyond the Wall, as they say in Berlin. Secretly, I was relieved she couldn't share that music with her school friends.

Let's be honest, Chris de Burgh wasn't exactly the pinnacle of '80s teen cool. I never fulfilled her request for a poster either. Jesus, none of us boys or girls, owned a poster of him!

Christian, on the other hand, was great for posters, mostly double-sided ones: Frankie Goes to Hollywood on one side, Michael Laudrup on the other. In fact, Michael Laudrup seemed to be on the flip side of everything, if I recall. Not bad for stamps either, Laudrup even ended up on one of those. Chris de Burgh, to my knowledge, never earned that accolade.

Anyway, those pen friends vanished pretty quickly. I clearly wasn't trekking to Poland to meet a girl behind the Iron Curtain, and eventually, my letters started getting returned, along with my confiscated mix tapes.

Christian, though? He probably stopped writing after showing up at Copenhagen Airport with his dad, waiting for me to arrive for a visit. I'd casually mentioned in a letter, "I'll be over next week, June

6th, suitcase stuffed with stamps, posters, and tapes!" But I never actually planned to go.

He must've taken it seriously. I did get a Christmas card that year, though, signed Christian and Michael.

Chapter 11 : Put 'em Under Pressure

Just heard Queen on the wireless, I think it was Queen anyway. They all sound the same these days, don't they? Still, it brought me back to Wembley and reminded me about the football.

Now, we all loved football, some more than others, but everyone supported an English team as well as their local Irish club. You could see the English teams on Match of the Day, but the only time you really saw Irish players on TV was when they played internationally.

All the lads followed a team: Leeds, Liverpool, Man Utd, Sunderland, and Ipswich Town were the main ones. Every now and then, there'd be an Irish lad playing for them, which always made it a bit more special.

Ireland qualified for the World Cup in 1990, for the first time ever. It's often seen as the moment our country grew up a bit, started getting noticed on the international stage. A little reminder to the world that our small island had plenty to offer.

Jesus, it was great craic. The whole country basically shut down whenever Ireland played. Everyone finished work early, unless your boss was a bollox. That gave you time to get to the pub and grab a seat, usually around the biggest TV in the area. They showed the matches on big screens too, that was a bit of a fad at the time. Odd the things you remember .

Funny thing was that most people had never been in a pub in the afternoon before. Any afternoon, really. Pints with your mates were for weekend nights, well they were for me anyway.

But for those matches, we'd head in early. Everyone wore an Ireland replica jersey, or at least a green shirt of some kind. Maybe an old Paddy's Day number, but whatever you had, you wore it with pride. You kind of assumed, in some daft way, that the team knew you were watching, that you were cheering them on.

Now, I don't believe for a second they actually knew we were dossing off work and drinking midweek in tribute to their success, but it felt like they did.

The team even hit number one in the music charts, if I recall. "Put 'Em Under Pressure", a daft song, but it became our anthem during the tournament. Well, the pub anthem anyway, sung from bars up and down the country.

While I'm at it, I remember that England, Egypt, and Holland couldn't beat us. Romania ,we won that one on penalties, with that Arsenal lad O'Leary scoring the decider. Then came Italy and that was the end of the road .

I remember it clearly because it was the first time I ever saw a whole table of drinks knocked over in a pub. Everyone had jumped up at once, kicking whatever was in front of them as Schillaci scored for the Italians.

And just like that, we were out.

We didn't have to wait too long for our next World Cup, that came a few years later, in the USA. I always thought that one was a bit daft. Football in America? Sure, I couldn't have named you any of their players. I do remember one ginger lad who fancied himself a rock star playing for them, though.

What I do know is their women's team was better than the men's. In fact, I think one of the players even ended up on the cover of Shoot magazine, showing off her bra or something like that.

What I do remember is getting our revenge on Italy. Ray Houghton scoring on a bloody hot day in New York, 1–0 to Ireland to kick off our campaign. That was our only win in the tournament, though. We went out in the second round to Holland.

It would be a while before we made it back again, in 2002, when, oddly enough, a lad called Holland scored our opening goal in that tournament.

Now that tournament, that's a story for another day.

Chapter 12 : Je T'aime

The biggest scandal when you were young was if the guards caught you robbing apples.

Our area had an endless supply of orchards or at least, I believed we did. We'd be out playing football all summer, and sooner or later, someone would inevitably boot the ball over a wall. Retrieving it was usually met with: "Jesus, there's an orchard in here!"

Robbing apples was the height of criminal activity back then. I was convinced that if they caught you, you were off to prison and when you finally got out years later, you'd have long hair, a filthy beard, and be wearing stripy pyjamas from one of those cells with bars and a flickering bulb that shorted every time it rained. The innocence of it all.

Then there was the other great scandal: The 'Who Left Mass Early' Scandal. This was a game played by most lads who were sick of going but still had to bring home proof for their mammies. You'd get grilled with: "Who said Mass?" (easily solved by peeking back inside) or "What was the Gospel about?" (another crisis avoided by nicking a look at the Sunday leaflet).

In fact, I'm convinced lads only stopped going to Mass when their mammies stopped giving out about it.

Maybe mothers are to blame for the fall in church attendance across the country, don't mind the dads; they didn't care whether you went or not.

And remember the fashion trend of stomping up the aisle for Communion in steel-tipped shoes? The unofficial "who can make the most noise" competition. That one never came back, odd, considering there's still plenty of shapers walking around the streets. They're missing a trick.

You'd also have to go to confession. You'd step into the confessional box, make the sign of the cross, and then proceed to invent a few sins to tell the priest, nothing too dramatic, just enough to sound believable. He'd then give you your penance punishment, two Hail Marys usually and all would be forgiven.

You always went with a mate so you could compare what you got.
"What did you get?" you'd ask, all innocent, with your halo on.
"Three Hail Marys and twelve Our Fathers."
I'd be thinking, Jesus, what the fuck did you tell him?

Another bit of petty crime? Smoking, back when it was still considered 'cool' and before we knew it was killing us. The local shop would sell looseys single cigarettes,

if you couldn't afford a full pack. You'd sneak one into the bill when your mam sent you for the messages. (The messages, what was that even about?)
"Pint of milk, a half-sliced pan, two slices of ham… and a loosey, please." Mam would be none the wiser. The things you got up to as a young teenager. I remember one of the lads used to squeeze the shite out of the bread to make sure he took the freshest bread back to the mother , an odd ritual but he done it all the same .

And of course, there was the sacred ritual of drinking a warm two-litre bottle of cider down some laneway before the junior disco. The lad who looked the oldest was sent into the off-license with a pocketful of coins, dumped it on the counter, and grabbed the nearest bottle, anything to get out fast before the shopkeeper started asking questions.

If only we'd known the cider in the fridge was colder and actually drinkable, we might've risked walking further in. But no, criminal masterminds, we were not.

The biggest scandal of all though, the one that really put us in mortal danger, was the blue movie incident.

Now, every gang had one lad who'd "found" a VHS belonging to someone who "knew somebody." Nobody ever admitted to actively looking for it, of course, no, it was always just found by accident. Word spread faster than anything else I can remember. Within an hour, twelve lads had somehow arranged to casually call over to someone's gaff for a glass of MiWadi.

I still remember the panic: sitting around a fuzzy old telly, curtains drawn like we were holding a séance. The video itself looked like it had been chewed up by the dog, the sound all over the place, some poor fella mumbling in German over a dodgy saxophone soundtrack.

Nobody spoke. We just sat there, half horrified, half trying not to laugh (or worse, look like we were enjoying it). Then suddenly, bang! The front door slammed. Someone's mam came home early.
Jesus! Madness! Delighted it wasn't my gaff. Lads diving over couches, one fella pulling the plug, another trying to eject the tape and nearly yanking the VCR off the shelf. We were out that door like someone had shouted, "The priest's coming!"

For weeks afterward, we couldn't look each other in the eye without laughing our arses off. As for the tape, it mysteriously disappeared. Some said it was burned. We all knew we'd seen things no twelve year, old really should.
But for some reason, every fella left that house walking a little taller.

Did it scar us? Probably not, but you best believe we all suddenly had an urgent interest in foreign cinema.

Chapter 13 : Saturday Night

Speaking of foreign .I'm lucky enough to recall some great holidays. In recent times , it's mostly bus holiday thingies, but I still remember our lads' holidays, especially the first one.

Some of the older lads from the area had already been to Spain, and we'd never hear the end of it. Stories about San Miguel being cheaper than red lemonade, lucky lucky men (I think they called them), bars and clubs open 'til 6 a.m., full Irish breakfasts in "Irish, only" cafés for a few quid, all the great lads they'd met and, of course, all the girls they'd kissed (or at least tried to).

And then there were the bloody holiday songs. You know the ones, some obscure track no one else had ever heard of . The in-joke song. They'd belt it out for the whole summer, swearing it was the greatest song ever made, and you just knew it'd be track one on the latest holiday mixtape, played to death before.

Now the local travel agent had a sign in the window, can't recall the price, but the picture was deadly. Anyhow, we went in, told her we wanted to go to Spain and experience what all the other lads had been raving about.

She looked at us and asked why lads like us would want to holiday with the golden oldies in Spain. Now, the other lads had conveniently left out the bit about the place being full of pensioners and newborn babies in buggies, bawling in the heat. No one mentioned we'd be sharing our dream holiday with half the contents of a retirement home and every family within a 40,mile radius.

So, she suggested we go to the Canaries.

The where? we thought. Sounded exotic, immediately out of our price range.

"Where's that?" we asked.

"Off the coast of Africa," she said. "A little party island off the coast of Africa."

Africa? What the fuck, I'm thinking. "We're not going to bloody Africa, we just want to go to Spain like everyone else!"

"It's owned by the Spanish," she said.

That gave us a bit of comfort somehow and that was that. A few weeks later, with our pockets jingling with pesetas and travellers cheques (remember those things?), we landed on the sunshine island of Gran Canaria.

Two drinks for the price of one, here we go !!

You judged your hotel room by the balcony, ours was overlooking the pool, six floors up. We'd sit out there every evening, drinking cans of San Miguel , talking absolute shite before heading into town to dance and drink the night away. These days they lock the balconies, health and safety, they say. Nonsense, I say.

Nobody believed in sun cream either. Not really. We'd slap on a bit of Factor 4 and wonder why we got roasted. Sunburnt legs in our Penney's shorts, and needing a few drinks just to numb the pain of putting shoes on, especially with the burn on the piggies.

The hotel room smelled like a mix of feet, coffee, after sun, lynx, pot noodles, crisps, cigarettes, alcohol and a splash of orange MiWadi someone had brought over "just in case." I think the cleaning lady gave up on us by day three. My room gets a deep clean these days .

Where were we supposed to put all the empty cans? Someone suggested the wardrobe, since none of us were actually using it. We all just lived out of our suitcases anyway. So that's exactly what we did: filled the wardrobe to the brim with empties. By the end of the holiday, it was packed to the top.

First impressions always mattered, well, they did on your first night out anyway. We were dressed like we were heading to a wedding: jeans "ironed" (well, more like squashed flat in the suitcase), hair gelled and hair sprayed within an inch of its life. One lad wore aftershave he'd nicked from his dad, though by the end of the holiday, we were all splashing on the old lad's cologne and promising to chip in for a dodgy bottle of Brut to replace it.

We'd walk into a pub or club that was three quarters empty but lit up like a rave, and we'd think we'd absolutely made it. Shots were dirt cheap, "buy one, get five" sort of thing . The place wouldn't come alive until hours later, but by then we'd be well oiled and ready to party.

You'd nearly always bump into a group of girls from Manchester or Glasgow in the same resort, but for some bloody reason, the Irish always stuck with the Irish. By the end of the holiday, there'd usually be some sort of gang formed, all partying together like old mates.

We'd try chatting them up with the usual bullshit charm, lies, and sunstroke. Claimed we were in a band, or semipro footballers, or once met someone who knew someone from Eastenders, some shite like that.

It almost worked!

Some cheesy Eurodance track played every night at the same time Dr. Albans "it's my life" or Whigfield's "Saturday Night", probably and it instantly became our anthem. We'd sing it on the walk home, on the beach, and months later in someone's gaff after a few cans. It made the holiday mixtape and haunted our parents for years. I loved holiday mix tapes

But somehow, you'd always end up in some dive bar listening to some fella belting out the holiday classic Alice. Alice, Alice, who the fuck is Alice? (What was all that about?) Then we'd all be up roaring Sweet Caroline or Bohemian Rhapsody.

Jesus, we murdered that song more times than I can count over the years.

We went to loads of places over the years, some I remember more than others. Mostly around Europe. I still bring my I Love Paris mug on holidays with me; it holds just the right amount of coffee from those machines. The handle's cracked, but it's been with me since… well, whenever.

I've a picture of the pyramids on my wall too, no idea why. Unless the Spanish own Egypt now as well as Africa.

Chapter 14 : Our House

I was looking for a postcard to send someone the other day, couldn't find any in the lobby. Then again, I don't even know where anyone lives anymore, with the new postcodes and all that.

The hotel I'm in now is all-inclusive. We used to dream of that kind of luxury, saying when we got older we'd spend winters away somewhere warm. Well, I've been here a few weeks now, and it's... grand.

I do miss wandering down the road for a proper Irish breakfast, but here I can help myself to anything I want in the mornings, so it saves the trip. Lavish spread, eggs Benedict, fresh croissants, proper orange juice. Can't complain.

Though the scrambled eggs taste like wallpaper paste. Must've hired a new chef.

The concierge brings me my newspaper every morning, first-class service. Her name's Janet (well, that's what her badge says) she then goes to meet someone down the beach for coffee most days . Nobody seems to be called José, Pedro, or Miguel anymore.

There's a few nice lads around too. We watch the football together in the recreation room, you know the place with the board listing the day's activities. No bar, but the lounge girls will always sort you out with a drink. I suppose that's what all-inclusive is for.

Satellite TV is also great these days isn't it . You don't even need to leave the hotel, the games are always on. Someone must've clocked I'm Irish because RTÉ seems to be on in the background most days.

And bingo , bingo is on tonight, that's usually a laugh, though it's mostly the women who play. Two fat ladies – 88 ! (Jesus did I say that out loud ?)

I reckon the younger ones are up on their balconies, having a few San Miguels before they go out , bingo for us older folk .

The winner gets the usual bottle of cheap Prosecco, tastes a bit like flat 7Up, if I'm honest. Not that it matters, it's usually shared around anyway. Never enough fancy glasses to go round, they're the plastic kind these days.

Everything's gone plastic now, hasn't it? Plastic glasses, plastic cups, plastic spoons. I think the place is afraid we'll claim if we cut ourselves on real glass. World's gone mad.

Best bit? The bar staff know the craic. They don't judge you for ordering a piña colada with your bingo card still in hand.

The entertainment at night is... well, it's something. Starts off with some poor young lad (think he's here for the holiday season) doing a quiz where half the answers are wrong, but nobody minds because we're three cocktails in and the questions are about old TV shows and pop songs from the '80s anyway.

Then comes the main act: maybe a fella on a keyboard who looks like he's been doing this circuit since the days of Live Aid, crooning out Elvis, Neil Diamond, and the odd Boyzone number for the younger crowd (that's us, apparently). He always throws in My Way near the end like he's headlining Vegas.

Some nights you get a magician, not bad, but you can see where the rabbit comes from and once a week there's a "Flamenco Night," which mostly involves a woman clapping and a lad in tight trousers shouting "Olé!" while we all clap politely between sips of sangria.

After that, it's over to karaoke. And Jesus, the same fella sings Delilah every week like it's the national anthem. Still, you have to admire the passion. Having said that I'm partial to an odd tune myself , I'll give any old song a go .

It gets a bit repetitive but hey we're here for a month or so not like it's a cheap and cheerful week in Benidorm.

One of the lads from Fr. Ted pops by a few times a week, asks if I want to go to his show at 9:30 in the morning. In the bloody morning , what's that all about . I know it's a posh place but that's Ott in my opinion . That's way too early for any singing and dancing at my age. I let the older ladies go, they seem to like it.

I just remembered I'll have to ask him where he gets his costume next time I see him, I think one of the lads' dads actually makes that sort of gear.

That reminds me, where's my walk ,man ? You can't get the radio on the bloody thing. I used to love tuning in for the Minute Quiz with yer man Larry Gogan. He always gets the honour of playing the first Christmas song on the wireless, before anyone else , before the other DJ's . Can't remember which one it was… probably that Mariah Carey one.

Haven't heard the quiz in ages. You know the one, where all the gobshites go on pretending they know everything but haven't a clue. They give answers like:

"What was Hitler's first name?"
"Heil."

"Where is the Taj Mahal?"
"Opposite the dental hospital."

And my personal favourite:

"What star do travellers follow?"
"Joe Dolan."

You couldn't make some of them up if you tried.

Then of course Movie night , sometimes afternoon depending on if the movie channel is on , Classics like Cocoon and Back to the Future, Robin Williams films , he's never in a bad one, a bit like Morgan Freeman , have you ever seen a bad Morgan Freeman movie.

Chapter 15 : Take My Breath Away

Remember when we'd go to the cinema to see the latest films? If nothing was on that jumped out at us, we'd try sneak into an 18 movie. Well, we'd send the tallest up to the counter to buy the tickets. The ticket seller never really cared if no one was around , we'd only be interrupting their magazine read , so 9 times out of 10, we'd get in.

Down the back, not to be kissing girls, but because we could smoke. Yep, puffed away, blowing all the smoke through the rest of the cinema. Little ashtrays on the back of the seats , madness now when you think about it. Blowing smoke up at the projector, hoping your cloud might be seen on the big screen.

You could get a beer in the cinema in England, which I always thought was brilliant, although I did get a glass of champagne once when I somehow ended up at a royal premiere , the Odeon in Leicester Square in London. Lady Di and I sharing the red carpet , I kid you not.

And the usher (nicknamed "The Torch" for his ever, present flashlight) would flash up to ye if we were making noise. Although silence, in fairness, was hard to find most of the time. You wanted to watch the film anyhow, and the shushes rang around the cinema only at the start. Then you'd relax into it, sharing your cigarettes and bon bons with everyone. Butts on yeh!

Some movies you recall for different reasons,

Batman, Terminator, Gladiator, typical lads' movies.

Top Gun, had to see in the cinema for the sound of fighter jets and Berlin's "Take My Breath Away."

Jaws 3D, yes, a third instalment. Just when you thought it was safe to get back in the water, nonsense. They made you wear glasses, one red eye, one green, that made you feel like you were in the dangerous water being chased by the shark. In truth, they were a bloody gimmick, and the movie relied on things flying at the screen, fish heads, harpoons, stupid special effects even for the time, and the novelty wore off very quickly. Proof God abandoned cinema in 1983

That was until Avatar, now that was a 3D movie. You felt you were in the bloody movie, though the glasses did make your eyes tired a bit, and the story was a bit like Pocahontas in space, to be honest.

The trailers were sometimes better than the film. We'd whisper to each other, 'We have to see that one!' Half the time we never did.

I recall using the ticket again once, we were just leaving Wayne's World, then "accidentally" wandered into Screen 3. Basic Instinct, with one of the lads , because he liked Michael Douglas , only to leave the cinema loving Sharon Stone after her crossing her legs and all that.

We went back a few days later and snuck into another 18 movie, as you do. No legs in this one , The Killing Fields. We left after a half hour , too serious , but walked into another one. Can't recall what it was called, but it was about this lad in Africa, middle of the jungle thing, gets hit with a bottle of Coca-Cola after the pilot of a plane flying over threw it out the window (I know), and it landed on this lad's head. He thought it was from the gods, and after a few attempts to figure out what it was , the village didn't like it , he was sent to find the end of the world and drop it over the edge. So we followed his travels with laughter. Funny as fuck, that was!

The Gods Must Be Crazy, that was it, bloody brilliant .

Ever go to the cinema on your own? It's a weird feeling. Billy no mates. Feel like everyone's looking at you, even though you're in the dark. I've done it a few times , not my thing.

Chapter 16 : Eye Of The Tiger

The wireless played that lad from Queen the other morning , sounding like someone from an opera, singing with some lady. "Barcelona." I remember watching with the lads in the pub, cheering on Michael Carruth as he won gold for Ireland in Barcelona. Gold medals , like bloody hens' teeth. It was a real moment of national pride. The airwaves played "Eye of the Tiger" to death.

Sonia was in the running too. I don't think she won a medal then, but she did at some stage. She won it all, didn't she?

I won a gold myself once , a few golds, actually. Didn't go to the Olympics though. The Olympic Committee declined my application. They didn't allow alternative sports back in those days , like the egg and spoon race, or the three legged race. Now they've got bloody table tennis, rock climbing, and diving.

(Diving , what's that all about? Getting high scores for tumbling into water? I don't know...)

Speaking of Eye of the Tiger , the Rocky films, they were brilliant. A local lad getting the chance to fight the world champion , mad stuff, really. Imagine that today , if one of the lads got into the ring with Mike Tyson, they'd be leaving in a box.

Rocky, though, did fight B.A. Baracus from The A-Team, and Drago , that Russian lad, a giant with muscles ,with the cool haircut that everyone had. And I think he also fought someone from Everton at some point.

Rocky went off to war in Vietnam or somewhere, I think , can't quite recall.

I think we had a Rocky mixtape as well , ah yeah, we did , for when we'd go on the walking machine things in the gym, or when the lads were trying to get muscles like Rocky or his Terminator mate. We'd be listening to songs like "Eye of the Tiger," Van Halen's "Jump," Snap's "The Power," and that one from the motor racing , ah, you know the one , the Fleetwood Mac one, "The Chain." That one got you focused.

Motor racing , or F1 as they call it now , I loved that. We'd watch it most Sunday afternoons. Jesus, it went on for hours. Cars going around in circles , well, not quite circles, and not figure eights like that Scalextric car racing game you played with as a kid. You know the one you always wanted but didn't get from Santa. The one you always dreamt of building in the attic because you'd seen some lad on the telly with a train set in his, and you thought, "I can do the same with cars."

Anyhow, nothing like that , F1 had loops, straights, corners, hairpins, chicanes... Funny, I don't know fuck all about normal cars, but I know F1. Well, at least I did , until they put it onto bloody Sky, like everything else.

We'd watch the Irish interest in F1 , they had Eddie Jordan, who owned Team Jordan. Yellow car, due to its sponsorship by the cigarette company B&H. Not the most glamorous or successful team, but deadly all the same.

Then you had Eddie Irvine , he drove for the red of Ferrari, the glamour car. Unfortunately for him, the world champion was driving the other Ferrari , Michael Schumacher , and he won most weeks. So Ireland's Eddie Irvine would settle for 2nd or 3rd in most races. A great achievement, but it didn't grab the headlines.

But the odd time he would win, the commentator would always get confused and call him British , but remember, he was Irish when he'd come 2nd. Odd lad not to remember that one.

Anyway, Eddie , he was a nice lad, sound. Bought me a drink once on a night out after we bumped into each other in town. Said there was a party back at his place , but I wasn't getting a taxi all the way to the bloody Southside where he lived. Would've cost a fortune. Nice gaff, I'd have guessed, though.

And I'll tell you where they had nice gaffs , Monaco. You'd see them hanging out of their windows as the Ferraris drove by at speed. The tiny principality transforms into a global party hub. The harbour fills with superyachts, the streets buzz with celebrities, and helicopters constantly ferry the ultra-rich.

I know a lad who goes , rents out a yacht between a few of them. Stupid money. They sleep and eat on the thing, but the mad bit is they watch the bloody race on a big telly on the boat, since they can't see everything from the harbour due to crowds and all. And the cars just zoom past anyway.

How the other half live , but in fairness, I'd want to be driving the bloody car for the amount of money the boat costs.

And Eddie Jordan , ah, I remember him playing drums on a night out in a dive bar in Coventry. Well, I think it was Coventry... That's the dead centre of England, right? Am I right?

Funny how sports glued us to screens and radios back then, nowadays, it's all Sky boxes and silence.

Chapter 17 : West End Girls

Quarter sticks of dynamite, they said they were. I'm not too sure myself, but they were the latest bangers on the market anyway, big bang. I mean, louder than anything we'd had before.

Halloween fireworks. And the gobshites would set them off during bloody daylight. They're for the dark, ye bleeding muppet, I'd be thinking, as the locals did their best to turn the area into Beirut a month before Halloween.

Fireworks were illegal to buy, probably still are, but I remember buying some as a teenager, from all places, the women on Moore Street. The sellers had them hidden under fruit and veg stalls, and sometimes under kids' prams if I recall rightly.

The police sort of knew, and mostly turned a blind eye, until their own kids wanted some. Then they'd go nab a seller, confiscate the fireworks... but bring them home instead of to the station. Allegedly, of course.

You'd buy a box of bangers, Benwell Bangers, from some woman who'd reach inside her coat, or more likely from under her apron, and produce a box of ten bangers while you kept sketch for the police. I kid you not.

Money would change hands, and then she'd ask, "Want any rockets, son?" They always called you son. It was like a trick question, really, because rockets just didn't fit in your pockets. You knew you'd have to stick them inside your jacket, probably down your sleeves and walk like a robot in case you bent and snapped one.

When I think about it now, I give a little giggle. How foolish we must have looked.

Sure, only a few weeks later, you'd probably be back buying your "three for two on the wrapping paper", from the same woman.

But fireworks were just the warm up act, Halloween night was the real show, there was the innocent ritual of calling to houses on Halloween night, dressed up and carrying a Quinnsworth plastic bag, hoping to fill it with apples and nuts from the neighbours. Great stuff.

We had no costumes back in those days. You wore a mask, no costume, just a mask that made it hard to breathe. You'd pull it up and down all night between knocking on doors. If you were lucky, the flimsy elastic band keeping it on would last the night. If not, you sort of held the mask up to your face.

You'd call at the door and say "Trick or treat", well, that's a bit of a lie. We said, "Help the Halloween party!" Some neighbours would ask who you were, we thought it was obvious: Dracula or Frankenstein, more than likely.

Most would give us the apples or nuts (nobody was allergic to them then) we expected, but the odd time you'd get money thrown into your bag, or, very occasionally, a sweet. I remember one year getting toffee apples from a neighbour, and from another chips wrapped in a cone made from the day before's Evening Herald.

I do recall answering the door one year, being told, "Now ask who it is" as I opened it. A young lad stood there, about five or six, I'd say. So I asked him, "Who are you, so?"

He gave me that look as if to say, Do you not recognise me? His face got sadder, his lips started to quiver, and just as he was about to bawl his eyes out, well, it looked like it, I was confused and concerned.

I was expecting him to say, "I'm Johnny from number 5," but instead he blurted out, "I'm Batman."

Of course he was.

I never asked any kid at the door who they were ever again. Lesson learned.

Nowadays, kids arrive in superhero suits bought online, shouting 'Trick or treat!' like they're in a Hollywood movie. But I'll always miss the days when Batman's identity crisis was the biggest drama on the road .

Chapter 18 : Walking In My Shoes

Janet sometimes forgets to bring the newspaper, but if she doesn't show, there's another nice lady who pops in a few times a week. She must have a good job, always nicely turned out (if you know what I mean)and she usually brings me something from her travels. A fridge magnet or a shot glass, that kind of thing. She must work away a bit, I think, but she's always busy. Last week she gave me a glass from Holland, Amsterdam, it said on it. The place sounds so familiar... I just can't place it though.

Football is on the telly most nights, so it must be that squeaky bum time near the end of the season. Squeaky bum time, I remember that Scottish lad with the big red nose saying that one night on the telly. One of the lads who pops in regularly, think he fixes computers and stuff for the place, always chats football with me. He's into my kind of music too, so that helps. Anyway, he told me that fella lost his job recently. I don't believe him though. I reckon he lost it after that 6–0 defeat to Ipswich years ago.

Another lady pops by too, lives nearby, I think. She's always up for a chat, can't shut her up sometimes. She's always "remember this" or "remember that." Always has headphones on her, looks the type who probably has a few mixtapes or playlists of her own.

Says she got her love of music from her dad. He must have had good taste. She often leaves me cakes too, says her sister bakes them. Well, I share them with the lads in here. Most of them have a secret stash of goodies in their rooms, so we swap. I've become quite partial to a bit of dark chocolate myself. Although if I see another packet of Milky Moos or Werther's Originals, we could open a bloody shop with the amount that goes around.

A lad they call "the butler" floats around ,offers dark chocolates at night while fluffing my pillows like he owns the bloody place ,not quite turn down service, but I know he means well. "Your fan club will be back tomorrow" "Who?" I said. He just laughed. I've heard him call me a resident once or twice, cheeky fucker, but he'll slip me the odd pill to help me sleep if the music down the corridor's too loud.

The physio bloke, the yoga instructor during morning activities, keeps telling me to "find my balance." Whatever the hell that means. I told him, "I'll use the Force.", it seemed the appropriate response , as I head for a swim after. They make me wear a bloody swimming hat also, what the fuck is that all about? They empty the swimming pool every night. Always thought that was a bit strange, but only found out why one evening when a few of the lads tried to go for a midnight dip. Not possible, it seems.
I did see some older lads on the telly the other night,

sneaking into a pool somewhere. Said it made them feel younger, stronger, full of energy. I'll have to find that one.

I need someone to look at my Walkman thingy, a tape got stuck in it the other afternoon. Don't mind, to be honest, it stopped on some rubbish song anyway. One of the lads, I think he works here, fixes the tills in the bar or something, popped by the other day. Gave me a few cassettes, said I might like them and that they'd jog a few memories. Shite, in fairness.
He also thought he was in the picture I have of my mates in the frame beside my bed. Don't be daft, I told him, these are my holiday lads.
He does have a box of screwdrivers though, so maybe he could have a look next time he's in.

Chapter 19 : Heroes

Every now and then you see someone in a mask, like COVID's made a comeback tour.
Remember COVID? I was off for about a year. We weren't allowed to work while dealing with the public and all that. Personally, I loved the time off. Okay, we didn't pay the mortgage for a while and nearly lost the business, but Jesus , it was a great break from reality. An escape, of sorts.

Now, I didn't find nature or religion or any of that kind of nonsense. But I did realise I'd been working since I was eighteen, and though I didn't see it at the time, I was burned out.

Obviously, I know COVID was different for everyone. It was very serious health-wise, and a lot of people died. But for me , it gave me a chance to recharge, in a way I didn't even know I needed.

For a while, time slowed down. Time moved differently. We had dinners together for a change, took walks, I discovered all the beautiful parks around me, reconnected with friends.

Those Zoom calls were brilliant. "Quiz Night," we called it. It was never really about the quiz , it was about being able to chat and see how everyone was doing.

Okay, we all learned a bit of useless information like: What colour was the first Lego brick? (Red.) Where was pizza invented? (Naples, Italy.) What was the first emoji? (A heart.) Stuff like that. But the quiz never mattered. It was about having a few beers on a Friday night with friends , a bit of normality. We'll have to do that again soon. I've a load of new questions to ask.

The walks were great too , they let me revisit loads of music, because nobody was releasing anything new at the time. I expected an avalanche of new music after, but it never really materialised, for whatever reason.

So: new headphones from Amazon (that was a discovery), and podcasts , now that's been a fantastic addition. And Spotify, obviously. A total game, changer. From mixtapes to playlists , the genius of it.

The discovery of new music is one of the greatest things , something that sounds familiar enough to what you usually like, but still different. Something new, but you just get it.

City streets that once buzzed went dead quiet. No pubs, no hugs , imagine, no hugs. It was a mad time.

Days did fly by, in fairness. Netflix filled a void for people. Contrary to popular belief, I didn't finish Netflix, but I did discover it's better to binge a series than to watch something week by week.

The last weekly thing I followed was probably Game of Thrones , though in fairness, it was the best TV show ever.
I do wonder, though , will yer man George Martin (not the fifth Beatle fella) ever finish writing the books? I'd like a different ending. (Spoiler alert.)

Remember, you couldn't go outside your area , ten-mile radius or something like that. So we walked the parks, walked the canals, even walked the beach a bit. Always ended up with a coffee from some pop, up van or another.

And baking bread , do you remember that? Bake Off on a budget!

Home, schooling was a weird one. Kids growing up without classmates. They don't even do sums the way we used to , what's that all about?

When we couldn't go out, music came to us , from balconies, from livestreams, from memories of gigs we never thought were our last.
The world stopped , and for once, everyone noticed. Even if we were apart, we were all going through it.

Some really, really shit things happened during that time too. Birthdays came and went unnoticed. Weddings postponed.
The missed goodbyes , people died alone. Screens replaced hands. Funerals had guest limits.
Elderly parents behind windows , what was that about?

We remembered what we missed , not the big stuff, but the small things: pints with friends (we don't do that enough , and the excuse that life gets in the way is valid, but it's still an excuse), a crowd, a crowd at a match, at a gig, at anything really.
Just missed crowds of people enjoying themselves, making new memories to never forget.

We were all stuck inside, but when I played Bowie, I was sixteen again. At least for a minute.

Chapter 20 : Being Boring

It feels like a lifetime ago we sold the old house and Dad moved into that little apartment by the coast. Now we have to sell that too, to help cover the care home. It's the right thing to do, we all agreed, but it still feels like another door closing. He went downhill quickly after Mam passed. I think his stories are his way of holding on, or maybe letting go. Maybe he needed to lose himself in the past because it hurt too much to stay in the present. Maybe he thought we'd be alright.

Some days, I'm not sure if he remembers her at all. Other days, he looks at me like I'm her and somehow, that's worse. On a recent visit, my sister and I sat with him, and for the first time in ages, he looked at us properly. He said we both looked like Mam. That we reminded him of her. Nothing more, nothing else, just that. Then he casually moved on, talking about some song or another.

He met mam in a club, I think it was the Galaxy club or something like that. Him and his bloody songs. He always said their song was Crazy for You. Used to drive us mad, how he'd hum it under his breath like some private joke we'd never fully understand. I only realised recently, that was the song playing when they danced for the first time. I think that was the night he knew he would marry her .

"He'll ask who you are," I tell the nurse. "Just say you're Anna from Poland. Or tell him you knew Mum. That always makes him smile. He said she could calm a room just by walking into it."

"I could listen to him tell stories every day. Half the time I don't know what's real and what's just memory dressed up a bit, but when his old friends visit and they visit a lot ,we all sit around listening, they nod along and say, 'That's exactly how it happened.' And for a while, I let myself believe it too. It's like he remembers more when they're here. Like some part of him comes back."

He does come back now and then, or at least it feels like he does. You'll be talking to him and suddenly, there's this spark in his eyes, like he's stepped through a door in his own mind and found his way back to us. I still ask his advice. I still value what he thinks. His opinions, they're still him, even if the rest of him drifts in and out.
I don't always know if it's really him I'm talking to… but I know he's in there somewhere.

Dad always used to say, 'When my time's up, it's up.' He had a million opinions on what might come after, he was never short on theories. I just hope he's not afraid now. I hope, somewhere deep down, he still holds onto the beliefs that once gave him peace. Though honestly… I doubt he remembers.

And the truth is, I don't really understand why his time isn't up yet. Don't get me wrong, I'm dreading the day it is. But this… this isn't how you should arrive at the finishing line. Not like this.

We found an old tape recorder, the one in his room now , while clearing out his apartment, along with a box of cassettes , about a hundred of them. Jesus, he must have loved making them. I knew he always had mix CDs in the car, and then that bloody iPod thingy , I don't think I ever saw him happier than when he was making playlist after playlist.

We found his 'Plague Tunes' CD , he named it after the covid pandemic beside his 'Live Aid 85' cassette . Both equally worn. Both equally real to him now

But I don't remember us ever having a tape recorder, only a CD player.
I thought maybe the tapes foolishly, would bring him back to us, jog his memory a bit .
Instead, they seem to take him further away.

While clearing out the apartment, we found a few bits I thought might jog his memory. The care home staff said we could decorate his room , add some personal touches. So we brought in a few old holiday souvenirs. He collected some real crap, to be honest.

There was a framed picture of the Pyramids , far too big for the skip , so we hung it on his wall. A massive mug from Paris, the kind that holds about three cups of tea. And a few old holiday snaps of him and his pals. We framed one of those and put it beside his bed.

He plays the tapes constantly now. Maybe to remember us. Maybe to remember here. Or maybe just to go back , back to sticky dancefloors, smuggled fireworks, and Ray Houghton's goal. Back when Madonna was queen and his hands didn't shake pressing play.

The nurses call it "agitation."

I call it migration.

He's rewinding through cassette doors, fleeing this quiet room for Galaxy Club lights. I watch him mouth "Crazy for You" to a nurse who wasn't born when it charted.

Press play. Rewind. Repeat.

This isn't remembering. This is reliving.

Printed in Dunstable, United Kingdom